THE
SHARD
RETRIEVER

VIRTUAL OR REALITY

RAYDAN ANGELO DEANE

AuthorHouse™
1663 Liberty Drive
Bloomington, IN 47403
www.authorhouse.com
Phone: 1 (800) 839-8640

Published by AuthorHouse 04/24/2019

ISBN: 978-1-7283-0337-6 (sc)
ISBN: 978-1-7283-0336-9 (e)

Library of Congress Control Number: 2019902002

Print information available on the last page.

This book is printed on acid-free paper.

authorHOUSE®

THE
SHARD
RETRIEVER

VIRTUAL OR REALITY

RAYDAN ANGELO
DEANE

CONTENTS

Chapter 1   Last Day of School 1

Chapter 2   Into The Game 9

Chapter 3   Image World 15

Chapter 4   Paradise 19

Chapter 5   Scaly Legend 25

Chapter 6   In the Real World 29

Chapter 7   The Blobs 35

Chapter 8   Prez 41

Chapter 9   Rescue Mission 49

Chapter 10   The Return To The Real World 53

FOREWORD

When people think about entrepreneurship, most tend to focus their thoughts on adults. I started my entrepreneurial journey as a teenager selling mixtapes. Growing up, I always had a love for solving problems, building relationships with people, and fulfilling my fullest potential in whatever area I put my mind to. When I look at Raydan, ever since he was a young scholar, I always noticed a different energy from him—an energy that reminded me of a young Jean. He is creative, smart, and ambitious. But more importantly, he loves his family and community.

One summer, Raydan spent a few weeks volunteering with me at Brooklyn Swirl, our frozen yogurt shop in Brooklyn. He wanted to learn how I operated the business and how I dealt with patrons on a daily basis. It impressed me so much because he wanted to do this all on his own. He is a self-starter and hungry for knowledge. Raydan was bitten by the entrepreneurship bug early. This book is just the beginning.

I want to take a moment to give credit to great parents who see the talent in their kids and allow them to pursue it young. As adults, I hope this book inspires you to listen to your kids. Let them create their stories, even though we know it's a hard road. Let them push along with our support. We must continue to invest not only in their education but in their dreams.

There are so many lessons in this book, and I'm confident that you will enjoy this read as much as I did. One more thing Raydan and anyone else reading this needs to remember is that regret is worse than fear. Always run toward your dreams. Don't let anyone hold you back. And if your dream isn't difficult to obtain, dream bigger!

God bless, and enjoy the read.

Jean Alerte | @MrAlerte

Award-Winning Entrepreneur and Author www.JeanAlerte.com

ACKNOWLEDGMENTS

So with my mother putting me through this invigorating journey, I give her huge thanks. She's a supermom and does all things I thought were impossible, including turning my punishment into this book. First she's sour then she's sweet, just like Sour Patch candy but much sweeter. She is the ultimate mother and a phenomenal leader. Her actions match her beliefs, which are very simple to follow: "A dream written down with a date becomes a goal, a goal broken down into steps becomes a plan, and a plan backed by actions becomes your reality." This is now my reality! Thank you, Mommy, Sudan Deane. I am so happy to see my thoughts come to life and to be able to share them with so many others.

I also thank my dad, Raymond Deane, for always taking time to speak to me about life and ensure that I am knowledgeable and will grow up with wisdom. I thank my uncle, Marqus Deane, for showing me the formulas to master the coding of computer science/technology. Thanks to my godfather, Phillip Hammond, for leading the way with the art of consistency, discipline, and his commitment to his passion of producing films and television commercials. Thanks to my uncle, Jean Alerte, for demonstrating the highest level of entrepreneurship and time management in running a successful brick-and-mortar yogurt shop in Brooklyn, New York. He's the author of two inspirational books and still found time to educate children on entrepreneurship in multiple schools. My grandparents—Carmen Deane, Egar Deane, and Angela Blair—have my thanks for always holding me accountable for my actions. And thanks to my little brother, Christian Deane, for always keeping me company and playing video games with me.

I am fortunate to have these great leaders and role models. If you are reading this book, then you are fortunate too because I am sharing what I've learned from them. As long as you are working toward your inner goal and dream, success is possible. The most important skill I learned from them was everything I do needs a plan and schedule. A plan doesn't just tell me what I want to do; it also tells me what I don't want to do. So the key to success on my journey is to have a clear plan.

CHAPTER 1

LAST DAY OF SCHOOL

A buzzer rings, and the clock says 8:30 a.m.

Cypher wakes up and mumbles under his breath, " Five more minutes," before falling back asleep. Then he wakes up and says, "Eight thirty! School is starting!"

"Oh, man, oh, man," he says as he heads to the bathroom.

Then he remembers it's the last day of school. So he takes a two-minute shower, puts on clothes, shoves toothpaste into his mouth, and brushes his teeth as he goes downstairs to get some cereal. He puts down the toothbrush, goes to the faucet, wobbles the water into his mouth, and spits it out. Then he forces the cereal into his mouth and puts the milk in there so he can finish his breakfast even faster. The second he swallows the cereal, he puts on his shoes, runs outside, and sees that he has missed the bus. So he has to run to the school.

Meanwhile at school, Ms. Thompson, the teacher, excitedly tells the class that it's the last day of school, and it's only a half day. The second she finishes her sentence, Cypher comes in.

Ms. Thompson says in a disgusted tone, "You're late. Get to work." Thirty minutes later, she tells the students, "Everyone open their books to page B52. Cypher, please read from the top of the page. Cypher … Cypher! Wake up! Wake up! Do you think it's funny to fall asleep in class? Well, do you?"

Startled, Cypher answers, "Yes, sir. I … I mean ma'am."

"Let's see what your mom has to say about this."

"But, but, but I didn't mean to—"

Ms. Thompson interrupts, saying, "But nothing. Go to the fifth grade across the hall."

On his way across the hall, he thinks, Just typical. Yep, my typical life at school. It's horrible right now, but everything is going to change since I have my VRH.

Twenty minutes later, the lunch bell rings. Cypher and a group of other kids get in line to go to the lunchroom. Once he arrives, he walks over to his best and only friend, Jimmy. He tells Jimmy he got the virtual reality gaming headset (VRH) that he wanted.

"Come over to my house tomorrow and we'll play it," Cypher says.

Jimmy answers, "You do know you have to pass, right?"

"Yes, I know. But I have faith I did."

Mr. Cherry, the lunchroom monitor, orders, "Line up for lunch."

When Cypher doesn't get in line, Jimmy asks, "You're not getting any lunch?"

"Nah, I'll just eat when I get home."

Jimmy nods and gets his food. But the second he gets to the table, it is time to go and get their report cards. Cypher runs over to the line. Jimmy literally throws the food in his mouth and runs over to the line as well.

Cypher sees his scores. He got a 70 percent in English, 80 percent in math, 90 percent in science, 50 percent in social studies, and 60 percent in health. On the top of the card it said, "You passed."

Cypher says, "Yes!" and runs home to play with his VRH.

Just as he's about to turn it on, his mom, Titania, asks, "What do you think you're doing? Did you forget you fell asleep in class?"

"No," he answers guiltily.

"Did you at least pass?"

"Of course!"

Titania responds, "Good. Since you passed, I'll let this slip. But I'll make a deal with you. I'll let you keep that piece of junk only if you promise to keep your room clean for the next two months. If that doesn't happen, then you are off. Understand?"

"Yes, I understand," he replies and then gives his mother a big hug.

"Do not forget. If that room gets dirty, I'm selling that piece of junk."

He plays the game for two weeks straight, and his room gets dirty. When his mom comes in and sees the dirty room, she turns off the game while he's playing it. Then she notices her son isn't moving. She looks at the helmet and sees a warning label: "Caution: Do not turn off console while in game."

CHAPTER 2

INTO THE GAME

Cypher goes into the game. In the sky it says, "Error: System turned off. Memory and data lost. Player trapped in game."

Cypher says, "Oh, come on. Wait, what?"

All the words in the sky flash and then disappear.

Cypher starts to flip out. "Wait, where am I? What's going on?" Something emerges from a shed behind him. Cypher turns around and is really scared. The thing looks like a regular man.

The man tells Cypher, "You are in the world of Virtual, a world where you are put throughout the depths of time and space, in many different universes."

"Dude, this isn't my game, Shard Retriever. It's a prank. Yeah ... yeah, a prank. So look, I just ... I just want to go home."

The man says, "Define your meaning of home."

"You don't know what a home is? What are you?"

The man replies, "I'm a cyborg named Vikksstry#18097. I ask again. What is your definition of home?"

"A home is, ummm, a place you live, eat, and do your business." Cypher paused.

Cyborg Vikksstry#18097 says "Your home will soon be revealed to you"

Cypher replies "Vikks number 172... listen cyborg... your names way too long, I'll just call you Vikk."

"New name processing complete. Call me Vikk," Vikk responds in a robotic voice.

"Okay, umm, what do I need to do? Do you know how to get me back home?"

"I do not know. But I do know you are Player 1, so just complete the game to 100 percent."

"All right. Let's do this."

"Okay," Vikk says, "first we are warping to a place called Earth."

"Earth? That's where I live. Wait, warp me there, and let's just go to my home."

"I am sorry, but I do not scan any places that you call homes on planet Earth. I did scan the shard on this planet."

"Let's just go and see if I can find any directions."

Vikk informs him, "Your objective is not to go home. It's to collect the Shard of Release."

"Okay. Let's just go."

"Get on top of that warp pad over there, and place your right hand on my left shoulder." As they transport, Vikk tells Cypher, "The Shard of Release gives you the ability to jump higher, see your mistakes in battle, warp, and move stealthier and faster."

"Cool."

After they arrive, Cypher asks, "Where do I look?"

"I do not know, but I do know you need to look inside that big object made out of—wait, processing— stones, bricks, metal, sandstone, and electric particles."

"That is what I would call a mansion."

"Okay, let's do the task at hand."

As the pair enters the mansion, an alarm goes off.

Panicked, Cypher says, "Wait; we are already busted."

Vikk orders Cypher, "Stop panicking and follow me." He punches through a vault and sees a shard just lying there. Vikk quickly picks it up and throws it at Cypher.

When the shard touches Cypher, he yells, "Ouch! Hot, hot. Very, very hot," and quickly throws it back at Vikk.

Vikk says, "I didn't teach you how to master it yet. So when we return, let me introduce you to a friend of mine."

The second Vikk finishes his sentence, police outside ask, "Do you want to do this the hard way or the easy way?" Vikk and Cypher run out of the mansion. The police officer said, "Of course, the hard way. We are in pursuit. I repeat, we are in pursuit. There has been a break-in, and thieves are on the run." The police get in the car and chase Cypher and Vikk. Almost a minute later, they corner Cypher and prepare to take him in.

Vikk runs in and picks up Cypher. As Vikk picks him up, the shard falls directly on his face. Vikk presses it against Cypher's face to get a grip on him. Cypher felt the same pain he would if an iron were being pressed against his face.

Cypher says, "Hot, hot, hot!" He grabs the shard from Vikk's hands and throws it. The police retrieve the shard and dispatch a team to arrest Cypher and Vikk and another team to take the shard to a safer place.

Vikk has no choice but to take Cypher and run, but not before marking the shard with his robotic eyes and seeing that the police have placed it behind a vault in a bank. They return to the shard-holder room where the collected shards are kept. Vikk tells Cypher to stay put. "I will come back for you." He gives Cypher a buzzer in case he is in trouble. Vikk leaves to return to the bank, but the police are outside protecting the shard, so he teleports through the bank door and the vault. The floor falls, and Vikk falls with it as soon as he grabbed the shard. He hits the ground and has to fend off all the police there, ready to shoot. He runs faster than the eye can see and knocks out every single one of them.

He returns with the shard.

CHAPTER 3

IMAGE WORLD

Vikk announces on his return that the mission was a success. "Now we head to a place named Image World, where you will learn to master the Shard of Release. So we will bring the shard with us."

Vikk and Cypher warp to Image World. When they arrive, Cypher sees he is standing above a place made entirely of clouds.

Cypher asks, "So where do we get started?"

"My friend will be teaching in the exact location you are in now."

"Where is he, then?"

"Directly in front of you."

Cypher sees a demon like creature in front of him. He gulps and asks, "Is that my teacher?"

"No, but the one behind him is." The first creature moves aside to reveal a cute cat sitting on the ground.

Cypher says, "Oh, that's such a cute kitty. So fluffy and adorable."

"This is your teacher."

"How could anything this adorable teach me to fight?"

The cat then turns into a muscular version of itself and warns, "If you call me adorable again, you will become cat food." Cypher gulps. The cat continues, "They call me KB, which stands for Kitty Boxer."

Vikk tells KB he has to teach Cypher how to use the Shard of Release.

KB responds, "Okay, let's begin. First, we need to go one full week without food, but you can have water. And I need you to copy exactly as I do."

Cypher copies KB by stretching, running, and sparring with him, making him go through straight-up torture. They do this for one week straight in the game, which is equivalent to twenty-four hours in real life.

The day after all the training, Cypher wakes up refreshed and feeling great. He drinks a gallon of water and throws a small portion of it on his face. KB throws the shard at Cypher almost at bullet speed. They start to spar, first by throwing and catching a whole bunch of rocks and then by jumping as high as they can. Before Cypher realizes, he is finally focusing on what the opponent is going to do and directing key energy into his stomach.

KB says, "Okay, you passed. You still need to work on your warping skills, but you're good enough to do the mission at hand."

Vikk informs Cypher, "The next place we are going is named Paradise."

CHAPTER 4

PARADISE

Vikk, KB, and Cypher warp to Paradise.

"So, where are we looking?" Cypher asks.

Vikk replies, "The shard is located next to the meditating old man. He is called Dog."

Cypher then hears a girl call out, "Help me," and runs over to her. She is locked in a cage. Cypher frees her, and Vikk quickly grabs the shard. Then the old man wakes up, grabs Vikk's arm, and throws him across the icy floor. Cypher runs for the shard, picks it up, and tries to escape. He is punched in the face and sent flying. Cypher passes out.

Vikk runs over to Dog and fights him. KB takes the girl, Cypher, and the shard back to the shard-holder room. When they warp, Vikk is left with Dog, who melts the ice Vikk is standing on. Vikk falls through it. Dog thinks Vikk is dead because all he can see is fog. Vikk teleports to the shard-holder room. Dog looks around for Vikk's corpse but soon finds that he has escaped.

When he returns, Vikk asks, "What should we do with the girl? Should we just leave her on the streets of Earth or keep her with us?"

KB replies, "Well, let's put her on the streets because I don't feel too good about this."

The girl steps up and says, "My name is Christina. Thank you for saving me back there. Could I be of any service to you? I have been trained in martial arts and judo. I can also see that you are probably collecting those shards, eh?"

Vikk replies, "Affirmative. But I don't believe you should assist us, so go and live out the rest of your life."

Cypher does not agree. "I think she can help us, so I'll stay with her and test her."

Vikk says, "Okay." Turning to Christina, he says, "I'll leave Cypher to test you."

Cypher tells Christina, "All right, let's start this thing."

Vikk says, "While you guys train, see if Christina can stay. KB and I will train. We cannot handle ourselves against the foe, Dog. So we will train."

Cypher goes to a virtual training room where he and Christina must fight and race.

Cypher says, "Come at me, and let's spar." Christina kicks Cypher directly in his face. He is sent flying and starts to bleed. Cypher charges at Christina and tries to land a punch on her, but she blocks each attempt.

Right as she was about to knock him out, Cypher says, "All right, all right, you can fight. Now let's begin the race." Cypher and Christina tie in the race. After the race, Cypher tells Christina, "All right, you are a very skilled fighter, so I think you could help assist us."

Once they leave the training room. Cypher calls out Vikk's name. Vikk and KB come out of their training room.

As Vikk walks out, he asks, "Did she pass?" Cypher nods.

Vikk says, "Okay. Our next objective is to go to a place named Antland."

The team transports to Antland. Vikk says, "Warning, stay away from giant ants." After they go through a giant door, Vikk announces, "Processing ... processing. Shard located under the rear end of the giant ant."

Cypher climbs on top of the giant ant. He collects the shard and throws it to Christina without waking the ant.

Christina runs to the giant door and shouts, "Yeah, sorry about this, but I have no more use for you!" She slams the door, waking up the giant ant.

Vikk says, "The ant is too dangerous to fight, so our only option is to escape." They run until they find a vent. But before Vikk gets inside, he scans it and sees it leads out through the door, and tons of giant bees are under them. They run through the vent, and the giant ant breaks through the door, waking the bees. The bees break out from under the ground, making Cypher, Vikk, and KB fly up with them. Christina looks behind her and sees a giant ant. The giant ant eats Christina and the shard but spits the shard back out almost the second it touches its tongue because it was too hot.

CHAPTER 5

SCALY LEGEND

When the survivors return to the shard-holder room, Cypher apologizes. "Guys, I'm sorry I brought Christina along with us." He looks at the sky and sees the game is at 67 percent. "Wait, so that was supposed to happen?"

Vikk says, "Forget about Christina. Let's move on to the next mission. We have to go to a place on Earth. You can see the humans, but they can't see or hear you. I warn you, though, that there are many types of dragons, so we have to go through some training."

Cypher, Vikk, and KB then go through a secret department of the shard-holder room. When they get there, Vikk tells Cypher to pick up three gallons of water and run fifty-two miles. Cypher does and comes back in an hour and twenty minutes. Vikk then says, "Now, hold eighty pounds of metal while running ten miles. Run forward and then back." Cypher comes back in thirty minutes, looking very exhausted.

Vikk says, "To conclude the training, fight me and KB." Vikk obviously beats up Cypher, but Cypher passes because he lasted more than twenty minutes against Vikk. Vikk then announces, "Cypher is ready to warp to earth."

When they arrive, Vikk says, "Processing ... processing. Complete shard found on top of material made of—wait, processing—wool, plastic, paper, and—"

Cypher cuts him off. "You mean the pillow?" Cypher runs and tries to take the shard. A giant dragon flies up and interrupts him. Cypher jumps back. The large dragon flies in a circle and becomes three medium- sized dragons. Each dragon picks one of them up and carries them into the air. The dragon that took Cypher throws him on a building, which cuts his arm. Cypher grabs the dragon and throws it across the air, making it fall right in front of the shard. Cypher jumps over the dragon and tries to reach for the shard. The second he grabs it, the dragon swallows him whole.

Vikk and KB, fighting their dragons, notice Cypher is missing. The dragon that fought Cypher goes over to help its dragon comrades. The dragons kick Vikk and KB to the floor, and the dragon that ate Cypher goes over to them and, using his sharp nails, tries to execute Vikk and KB.

Cypher rudely interrupts this by vibrating his body to make it reach a very hot temperature. He literally becomes a ball of fire inside the dragon, destroying it from the inside out. The other dragons wonder what's going on. Once Cypher melts the dragon into a ball of fire, he throws it at the other dragons, which eradicates them as well. Cypher takes the shard to the shard-holder room.

CHAPTER 6

IN THE REAL WORLD

Meanwhile in the real world, Titania, Cypher's mom, discovers her son can't physically hear, sleep, see, eat, or show any signs of consciousness. She immediately brings Cypher to the hospital. After their examination, the doctors say, "Your son is in some type of a numb state. How exactly did this happen?"

Distressed, Titania says, "I just unplugged the game because he couldn't hear me. I kept calling his name but he wasn't responding, so I knocked the headset off his face. He was non responsive! He had a blank look to his face, my baby boy was completely gone!"

Titania starts breathing heavily and says "I feel like I did this, the smack must of triggered this."

One of the doctors says, "We ran some tests and your son doesn't seem to show any signs of trauma. Oddly enough he's actually in pretty good condition, all of us have never seen anything like this ever before. I would assume that this is a coma but it's different, something new entirely. In school we are taught that for every effect there is a cause, but there is no cause for this incident. Don't worry Ms. Titania, you have nothing to do with this incident."

"Okay" Titania says, She then takes a deep breath, stands up, looks the doctor in the face and says "Are you saying that you can't bring my baby back?" The doctor says "We will try everything we can."

For the next two weeks Titania stayed by her son's bedside hoping and praying for her son to wake up. Brokenhearted, Titania finally goes home. She tries to fight back her emotions but she looked on her wall and saw a picture of Cypher's father, a baby Cypher and herself. She breaks down letting all of her emotions come out falling down to the ground, but then she sees Cypher's baby face smiling. Crying she says "I can't lose you too, please give me a sign".

Frantically she gets up, with tears in her eyes and begins to search the internet for answers for unexplainable comas. After hours of searching, she finds a video from an online conspiracist.

It was titled "Beware of the video game The Shard Retriever."

The video opens up with a man that is sitting in a dirty chair, the man didn't look normal as his face seemed pretty pale and he looked very scared.

In the video he claims that the creators of The Shard Retriever have a global conspiracy to take over the minds of all the children of the world.

Titania was about to turn off the video dismissing it as ridiculous but then the man in the video says this "If anyone you know goes into a coma while playing this game, contact me as soon as possible because the fate of humanity lies in their hands."

He pulls the camera closer to his face and says " This is not a joke!" I repeat if you know someone who has gone into a coma playing The Shard Retriever contact me, this person is very special and the fate of the world depends on it."

Titania goes into the description of the video and finds out where to contact him.

She then messages him through his email telling him her story. Within seconds she gets an email back from him with instructions to video call him.

She video calls him and he picks up instantly. The conspiracists Pat says "Titania we don't have much time so you have to listen to me very carefully okay." Then Titania replies "Yes please tell me what's happening to my son."

"Your son is in a lot of danger! We all are! Right now he is stuck in a game and if we don't help him get out he can be stuck there for eternity. Go and get the headset that came with the game immediately."

Titania brings Cyphers headset over to show it to the camera.

Pat says in a fast manner "I want you to listen to me very carefully okay, I am going to give you a cheat code to put into the game that will allow him to progress in the game faster. If he completes the game he can come back to the real world, but if you mess up you will cause him to glitch in the game. This will roughly drop his chances of winning to a 35% chance alright. Now turn on the headset."

Titania turns on the headset. The light on the top shines.

Pat says to press in the top left, and pull out the mini keyboard that is inside of it. Titania does this and says "how did they manage to fit this in here"

Pat says "Focus. Okay this is the really important part of this whole sequence. DO NOT MESS UP BECAUSE IT'S OUR ONLY CHANCE ON SAVING Cypher. On the controller press X-A-B-YB."

Titania says "ok I did it"

Pat says "now press d-f…." suddenly Titania hears an explosion in Pat's apartment!

Pat's door blasts open and men in Swat gear scream "GET ON THE GROUND!!" Pat jumps out the window as the swat team shoot up the laptop disconnecting Titania and Pat.

With the connection lost, it left Titania with even more questions than answers. How was the fate of humanity in her son's hands? Why would a swat team invade Pat's apartment? As puzzled and confused as she was. She knew no one would believe her so the only thing she could do is pray for the return of her son.

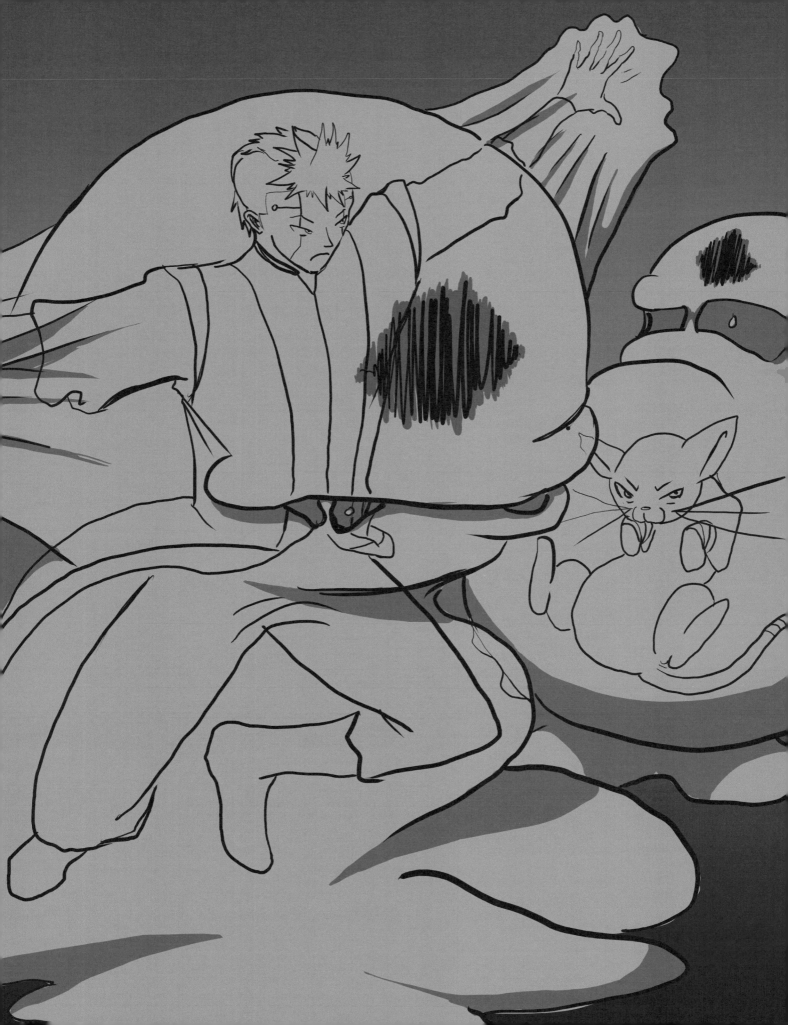

CHAPTER 7

THE BLOBS

When Cypher tries to warp back to the shard-holder room, he glitches. Vikk has to grab him.

When they arrive, KB says, "I think you should stay back because you were kind of glitching back there. Do you know what's causing it?"

Cypher answers, "I think my mom is probably trying to help fix my problem."

KB says, "Oh, all right. I still think you should stay back just in case anything bad happens."

Cypher understands, and they prepare to go without him.

Vikk asks Cypher, "Remember that buzzer I gave you around the same time we met?" Cypher nods and looks at his wrist. "If the buzzer rings, it means we are in trouble. We can also talk through it."

Cypher says okay and sits down as Vikk and KB say goodbye and warp to a world called Crets.

When they arrive, Vikk says, "Processing ... processing. Shard is located on that pillar over there." KB picks it up, and Vikk replaces it with a decoy. Just as Vikk finishes the job and he and KB try to run away, a group of blobs surround them. The blobs stand and stare at Vikk and KB. Vikk approaches one of the blobs and tries to punch it, but his hand gets stuck in the blob's body. Soon, Vikk's whole body is absorbed. The blobs crowd around and fall on top of KB, absorbing him as well. They spit them out and handcuffed them, preparing Vikk and KB to be hanged.

Then the buzzer Vikk gave Cypher goes off. Cypher starts warping to meet and help his friends. While he is warping, Vikk speaks through the buzzer, "Cypher, do not touch the green organisms, or they will absorb you. Make a plan before you rescue us. The green organisms love to keep hold of dangerous materials in their—what do you call them?—homes."

"Okay, I'll make a plan." When Cypher arrives, he spots a house. When he investigates, he sees a lot of explosives, a rope, and a match. I need to lead those green organisms to the explosives, he thinks. He calls Vikk back on the wrist buzzer and asks, "Where are you, Vikk?"

Vikk answers, "I do not know. Where are you?"

Cypher answers, "I'm on a street named BzZzerf Street."

Vikk says, "Processing ... processing. Go straight, take a left, and then climb over the brick wall."

Cypher follows the instructions and finds Vikk and KB tied up on the floor with some weird rope. He tries to untie them without being spotted. None of the blobs see him. Though Vikk tries to warn him against it, Cypher tries cutting the rope. All the blobs are alerted. The blobs hop on each other and become a really big blob. When Cypher, Vikk, and KB escape, the giant blob is right in front of them.

Cypher and the group run for their lives. "Follow me. I have a plan," Cypher shouts.

Vikk responds, "Affirmative. When you cut the rope back there, the blobs sent their troops to guard the shard more closely."

"How did you hear that would happen?" KB asks.

"I am a cyborg," Vikk replies. "I can understand any language and translate it to any one of the other languages across all universes."

Cypher says, "Okay, the house is right there. Follow me."

The blob struggles to get into the home but finally forces itself in. Cypher goes to the basement, puts the rope around the explosives, and lights it with the match.

Vikk warns, "We have approximately twenty seconds to escape to a range of one mile." Cypher, Vikk, and KB scramble out of the building, leaving the giant blob inside. Cypher and the group run as fast as they can to get out of the blast radius. They succeed, and all the explosives in the city blow up.

Cypher says, "All right! We did it again. Vikk, where is the shard?"

"Did you forget that I said the blobs sent other troops to properly guard the shard from us?"

Cypher asks, "Oh, come on, I did all this for no reason?"

Vikk answers, "Affirmative."

KB chimes in. "Show us the way to the shard, Vikk."

Vikk guides the team back to the shard. When they arrive, they see five blobs guarding the shard.

Quietly, Cypher asks, "What's the plan?"

Vikk says, "KB, you run over there and draw the blobs' attention. I'm guessing at least two will stay to watch over the shard. Cypher, I need you to take that shard and throw it at one of the blobs."

"Won't they absorb it?" Cypher asks.

Vikk answers, "Yes, but they will spit it back out."

"On three we go: one ... two ... three! Go!" KB runs and draws the blobs' attention. Cypher grabs the shard and throws it at a blob. The blob absorbs it and throws it at the other blob right next to it. That blob spits it out, and Cypher catches it. All the blobs fall to the floor. KB outruns them, Cypher takes the shard, and Vikk just watches. Then the team warps back to the shard-holder room.

CHAPTER 8:

PREZ

Back in the shard-holder room, Vikk suggests, "I think you should come with us to the next world, which we call Prez. You've proven that you are just as strong as either of us."

Cypher responds, "Really?"

Vikk answers, "Yes. But that's enough for now. We need to focus on the task at hand."

Cypher asks, "So what is this Prez place, and do you know what we are up against?"

"Negative. The only data I have in my memory is that people call it a dream world."

"All right," KB says, "let's just go."

In Prez, Vikk, KB, and Cypher see everything they've ever wanted and ever dreamed of. Vikk sees a bed. KB sees kitty toys and the biggest fish in the world. Cypher sees a chocolate fountain, ice cream, every game he ever wanted, toys, a high school diploma, beautiful women, and puppies. Cypher and KB run toward the things they've always wanted. KB takes a bite of the fish, and Cypher pets the puppies.

As they did so, everything becomes terrifying. The fish gets moldy and has maggots. The puppies turn into wolves, and the beautiful women turn into ugly witches. Vikk's bed is cut in half and becomes Dog, the old man who beat up Vikk, Cypher, and KB a while back. Dog gets out and taps Vikk on the head, and Vikk falls on the floor and breaks apart. The wolves and witches knock out Cypher, and KB gets tremendous food poisoning. Then they all lose consciousness.

When they awake, they are being hanged, including Vikk who had automatically reassembled himself with his robotic programming.

Cypher asks, "Well, is there a way for us to escape?"

"Negative. There is no way for us to escape," Vikk admits.

As he finishes his sentence. Cypher phases through the ropes and quickly works to untie them. As he does, he asks, "Where is the shard?"

Vikk answers, "In the middle of KB's disgusting fish."

Cypher sees the shard in the fish full of maggots, which was being protected by some lions. Cypher runs toward it. When he picks it up, the wolves and lions tackle him. Cypher kicks a wolf and throws the shard at a lion. A witch casts a spell that locks Cypher in a cage that is set to detonate in ten minutes. The only way to get him out is to kill the witch. The witch snaps her fingers, and KB drops to his knees and begs for water because he has the world's worst stomach ache. Vikk runs at the witch and attempts to punch her. Before his fist can touch her face, she turns the floor into ice and then shatters it. The witch holds Vikk in the air, and he can't move. She picks up a bottle of poison and says, "Well look, you're running out of time." Vikk sees the timer on the top of Cypher's cage reads only two minutes.

The witch throws the bottle of poison at Vikk. He uses his hands to stop the glass from breaking and throws it back, striking the witch and shattering. The witch burns and cries, but the timer still counts down. But once it reaches just one second left, it stops. The cage opens, releasing Cypher. Dog comes and uses an energy pulse to push Cypher, Vikk, and KB.

When Cypher opens his eyes and the fog disappears, he sees he is in Paradise, the place where they had first met dog. Then he sees the shard just lying on the ground in front of him. He picks it up and sees Dog's hand about to punch him. Vikk takes the punch, shattering his human like face and leaving just his metal skull. KB grabs Cypher and says, "I'm sorry, but we have to leave him. I swear we will come back for him." So they warp back to the shard-holder room.

Meanwhile, Dog picks up Vikk with one hand and punches him with the other.

Dog tells him, "I am going to make you suffer."

CHAPTER 9

RESCUE MISSION

In the shard-holder room, Cypher looks at the sky and sees he's at 95 percent.

Then they set out on a rescue mission to save Vikk. Once they get back to Paradise, KB and Cypher help Vikk to fight Dog. They punch Dog really hard, sending him flying and leaving him to bleed. Vikk jumps on him and scratches his face. They kick him over and over until Dog breaks through the ice below them. Cypher uses the fireball move he learned earlier and throws it at Dog. All they can see is fog. But Dog comes out with bruises and cuts. Vikk, KB, and Cypher punch him again really hard. They then walk away, thinking they won.

Suddenly, Dog grabs Cypher. "I'm not going down without taking at least one of you down with me. In ten seconds, I'm going to blow up and create an explosion the size of a nuke."

But Vikk punches Dog and grabs him in an armlock. He quickly tells KB to teleport to the shard-holder room. Before they go, Vikk tells Cypher, "You've become a great fighter, and I wish you the best of luck. All I can say is that you need to treat every day as if it were your last."

Cypher mumbles under his breath, "Yes, I will."

When Cypher and KB return to the shard-holder room, in the sky it says, "Game at 100 percent." Cypher flies into the sky and returns to the real world.

Vikk sacrifices himself to Dog for the greater good.

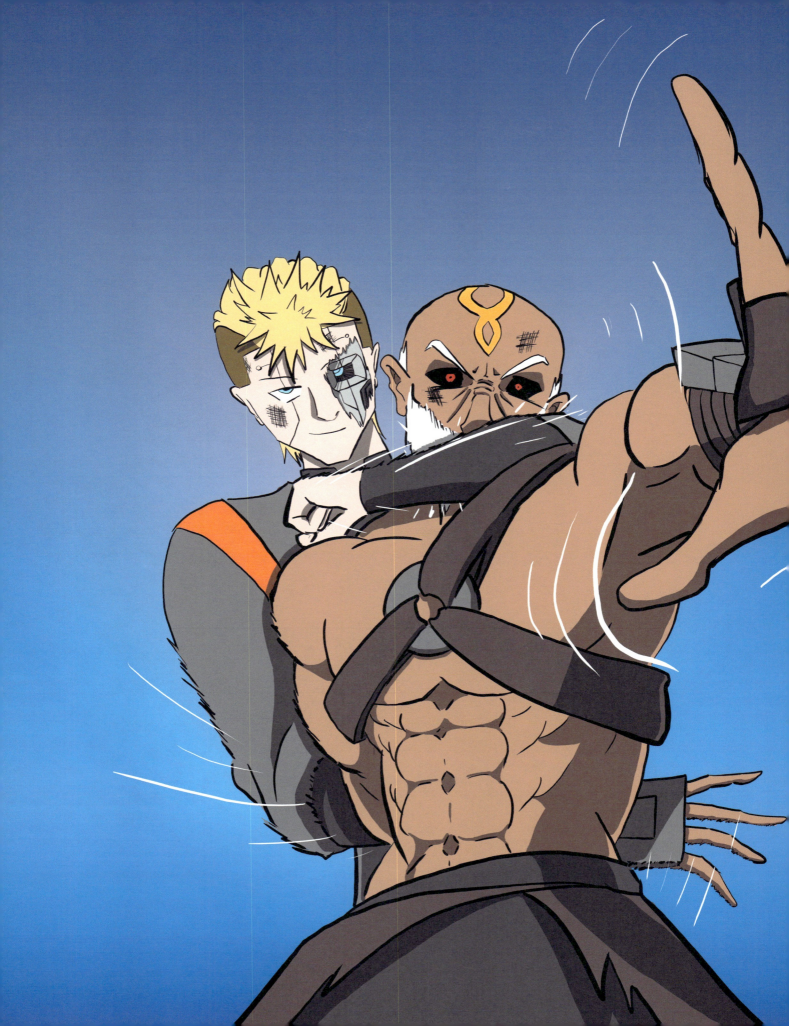

CHAPTER 10

THE RETURN TO THE REAL WORLD

When Cypher returns, he wakes up in his mother's arms. She cries as she gives him a huge hug. She says, "I'm terribly sorry I made you go through all that trouble."

Cypher says, "It's okay."

Titania says, "I'll do anything to make it up to you. Anything, especially after the weird interaction I had with a conspiracist named Pat." Cypher says "Wait, what conspiracist?" Titania says "That's a topic for another day, right now I am just happy you are alive and in my arms again. Now tell me what would you like?"

Cypher thinks, "Well now, I could get almost anything I want." But then he remembers that if he kept his room clean, none of this would have happened, and his mother would not have gone through this stress.

So he takes responsibility. "It wasn't your fault that I didn't keep my room clean. And I'm pretty sure you didn't know that turning off the game while I was playing it would trap me in there. I have so much to tell you about the experience I had." For a second Titania wondered if there was some truth to Pat's story after all. But the thought of it all was just so overwhelming. Her only focus now is to keep Cypher happy and safe. So she replied as if she was still in denial "Well, it's my job as an adult to take care of you, and I did the exact opposite. What type of mother would trap her own flesh and blood in a video game? So please, can you just tell me what you want so I can make it up to you?"

"Okay, my wish is for you to just be yourself."

Titania quietly says, "I'll do that for you."

Cypher jumps off the bed and tries to warp downstairs. Then he remembers he isn't in the game anymore. As Cypher falls to the floor, the doctor in the room says, "Well, I'm sure he doesn't have any of the powers he had in the game."

Cypher returns home with his mom. He goes online to see if there is a way to become as powerful as he was in the game. He finds a video and starts to copy the man showing him stretches and body workouts. He continues to do this for the rest of the summer. Next year, he returns to school looking really buff. When he gets there, everyone stares at him and asks about how he became so buff. He tells them how he did it and grows up to make a living doing so. He tells his story on all forms of media and starts to live a great life.

One day, he was working out in the park and he hears a robotic voice say, "Congratulations Cypher." Cypher turns around and sees Vikk. Out of pure astonishment, Cypher says, "How are you here? How are you even alive? Are you real? Is this place even real, or am I still in the game?" Vikk says in his robotic voice " The game has just begun."

TESTIMONIALS

Raydan has a mind and personality beyond his adolescence. Throughout his early childhood years, he regularly engaged me in meaningful and thought-provoking conversations. I am so proud of the young man he has grown into, and that he has successfully married his creative mind and entrepreneurial spirit into every page of this book. Shard Retriever: Virtual Or Reality offers children who love gaming a nice escape from the monitor and controllers and offers parents a meaningful window into the mind of a child obsessed with video games.

—Phillip Hammond, Godfather

I am incredibly proud of this story. While it was not the self-evaluation formulas I was expecting from my son, I was totally blown away by his creative writing skills. Raydan's story captivated me on such a level that I was engulfed in each chapter, literally imagining the scenes as if I was watching a movie.

This story was encouraging not only for me but also for my son. Our bond grew stronger and I continue to support and assist with his visions and dreams.

Raydan is extremely creative and grasps the concepts of things easily. However, through his creativity I've learned that it is important to engage him in meaningful conversations and hold him accountable for his actions and commitments. Raydan has weaknesses of his own, like staying focused on one thing at a time before racing to the next. Through conversations with him, I learned very quickly that my son is a young visionary. In order to help him see his visions through, I gave him two books: one book to write down his visions so he never loses his thought or ideas, which serves as a checklist, and a second book to create the plan constructed with a date of completion. Then I follow up periodically and also incorporate each task's projected date of completion on my calendar to ensure accountability. This method keeps Raydan organized and on track before moving on to the next grand idea without losing his vision. Through this concept, I believe I am keeping my son focused and he's learning the right behaviors and developing the right skill set needed to find his mastery. I certainly identify a skill my son poses and enjoyed the read and hope you will also.

—Sudan Deane, Mother

Raydan, I tell you all the time that you're a billionaire. That is because you have a creative ability to imagine the most amazing stories and business ideas. You are the definition of a creator. Your first book, The Shard Retriever: Virtual or Reality, proves how imaginative you are. You wrote the book with ease. And even more impressively, you wrote it at age ten. I know you have many books, movies, and businesses that you are excited to create. Everything you do will be a tremendous success, and I'm very proud of you.

—Raymond Deane, Father

Raydan, continue to listen with curiosity, speak with honesty, and act with integrity. Always remember that behind every successful coder is an even more successful decoder to understand that code behind an even better masterpiece. My message to you will always be, "Give a man a truth, and he will think for a day. Teach a man to reason, he will think for a lifetime." That's the successful method to cracking any code or sharpening your skills in anything you do. Lastly, listen to people who are wiser than you. That way, you don't repeat the same mistakes they did.

—Maques Deane, Uncle

ABOUT THE AUTHOR

At age ten, Raydan Angelo Deane's mom, Sudan Deane, had enough of his messy room and atrocious report card from school. So she decided to ground Raydan by taking away his gaming systems and have him fill an entire college composition book—front to back—with plans of how he could improve his grades and keep his room clean.

To her surprise, Raydan wrote a very exciting and captivating novel that takes readers on a wild and exciting journey. It follows the adventures of a boy named Cypher, who has to gather the scattered seven pieces of the Shard of Release to complete a game he is trapped in. This is the only way Cypher can come back to his mother in the real world.

According to Raydan, he decided to write a story that shows parents what makes kids love games so much and, in a way, show kids what entertainment can do to their minds.

Think about it this way: what happens when you break down the syllables in en-ter-tain-ment? It's like saying enter, tain/attain/tame it, and ment (short for mental—aka the mind). Now the problem with entertainment is that it's fun, but as shown in the story, bad things can happen if you let it tame your mind.

ABOUT THE ILLUSTRATOR

Illustrator Mal Xanders of Advent Media Works was born and raised in New York City. He specializes in character design and conceptual art.

ABOUT THE BOOK

Follow the mysterious and magical journey of a boy named Cypher whose mind is accidentally trapped into **"The Shard Retriever"** the world's #1 virtual reality video game. While Cyphers mind is stuck in the game, it leaves his body paralyzed and his mother devastated searching for a way to revive her son.

How can Cypher return to the real world?

The only way Cypher can return to his mother in the real world is by completing the game to 100 percent. Cypher must retrieve the seven pieces of the Universal Shard scattered on planets guarded by giant bees, disgusting blobs, scary witches, ferocious wolves and fire breathing dragons! Luckily he has the help of a cyborg and a Kitty Boxer … *whatever you do, just don't call it a cat!*